This Topsy and Tim
book belongs to

_____

go to the zoo

Jean and Gareth Adamson

All Ladybird books are available at most bookshops, supermarkets
and newsagents, or can be ordered direct from:
Ladybird Postal Sales PO Box 133 Paignton TQ3 2YP England
Telephone: (+44) 01803 554761   *Fax:* (+44) 01803 663394
A catalogue record for this book is available from the British Library

Published by Ladybird Books Ltd
A subsidiary of the Penguin Group
A Pearson Company

Topsy and Tim were going to the zoo.
First they made sure their pets had
all they needed for their day at home.
'Let's ask the zoo animals if they
would like to come home with us,'
said Topsy.
'Animals can't answer questions!'
said Tim.

Topsy and Tim met the penguins first.
They walked like funny old men
but they dived and swam beautifully.
Topsy and Tim would have liked
the penguins to come home with them
but they looked so happy in the zoo.

The parrots in the aviary were making
a dreadful noise. Topsy had heard
that parrots could answer questions,
so she asked one, 'Would you like
to come home with us?'
'Ripe bananas, brown bread,'
squawked the parrot.
'I'm afraid parrots don't give
sensible answers,' said Dad.

They took a ride on the elephant's back.
'We're the highest in the whole zoo,' said Tim.
Then they saw a giraffe. She was higher still,
although her feet were on the ground.

'Look!' said Tim. 'Horses in football jerseys.'
The zebras showed how they could kick.
One kicked another with his back hooves.
'We don't want those zebras at home,'
said Dad. 'They might kick *us*.'

'Look! White teddy bears!' said Topsy.
'Those are polar bears,' said Mummy,
'and they are very fierce.'
'We won't take them home,' said Tim.

A crowd of people hurried past Topsy and Tim.
'They are going to watch the lions being fed,'
said Mummy.
'Let's go too!' shouted Topsy and Tim.

LITTER

The keeper brought huge lumps of meat for the lions. It was fun to see them enjoying their food.

Topsy and Tim were hungry.
Mummy found a slot-machine
that sold orange drinks and chocolate.
Topsy and Tim thought it was a
good slot-machine.

The sea-lions were hungry too. The keeper
threw them fish from a bucket.
'Can we take a sea-lion home?' asked Tim.
'No,' said Topsy. 'It might eat our goldfish.'

Topsy and Tim wanted to take all the
monkeys home. But it was time for Mummy
and Dad to take Topsy and Tim home.

Topsy and Tim were glad they had not
brought any zoo animals home. Their own
pet animals were just as interesting
and they were good old friends too.

'I don't know why we go to the zoo,'
said Dad. 'We've got our own zoo
at home.'